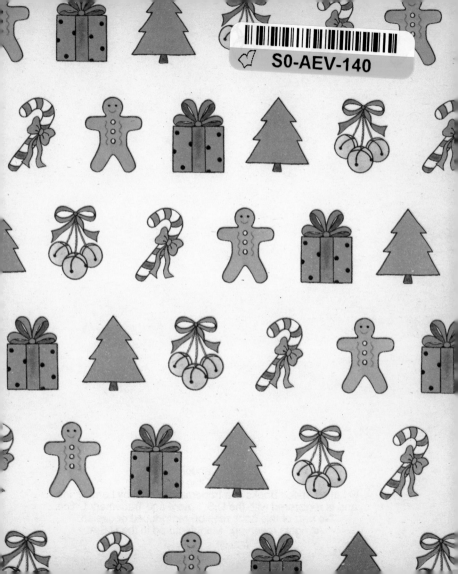

The Twelve Days of
Christmas

On the first day of Christmas, my true love gave to me, a partridge in a pear tree.

On the second day of Christmas,
my true love gave to me,
two turtle doves,
and a partridge
in a pear tree.

On the third day of Christmas, my true love gave to me, three French hens, two turtle doves, and a partridge in a pear tree.

On the fourth day of Christmas, my true love gave to me, four coly birds, three French hens, two turtle doves, and a partridge in a pear tree.

On the fifth day of Christmas,
my true love gave to me,
five gold rings! Four coly
birds, three French hens,
two turtle doves,
and a partridge
in a pear tree.

On the sixth day of Christmas, my true love gave to me, six geese a'laying, five gold rings! Four coly birds, three French hens, two turtle doves, and a partridge in a pear tree.

On the seventh day of Christmas, my true love gave to me, seven swans a'swimming, six geese a'laying, five gold rings! Four coly birds, three French hens, two turtle doves, and a partridge in a pear tree.

On the eighth day of Christmas, my true love gave to me, eight maids a'milking, seven swans a'swimming, six geese a'laying, five gold rings! Four coly birds, three French hens, two turtle doves, and a partridge in a pear tree.

On the ninth day of Christmas, my true love gave to me, nine ladies dancing, eight maids a'milking, seven swans a'swimming, six geese a'laying, five gold rings!
Four coly birds, three French hens, two turtle doves, and a partridge in a pear tree.

On the tenth day of Christmas, my true love gave to me, ten lords a'leaping, nine ladies dancing, eight maids a'milking, seven swans a'swimming, six geese a'laying, five gold rings! Four coly birds, three French hens, two turtle doves, and a partridge in a pear tree.

On the eleventh day of Christm
my true love gave to me, eleven piper
piping, ten lords a'leaping, nine ladies
dancing, eight maids a'milking...

...seven swans a'swimming, six geese a'laying, five gold rings! Four coly birds, three French hens, two turtle doves, and a partridge in a pear tree.

On the twelfth day of Christmas, my true love gave to me, twelve drummers drumming, eleven pipers piping, ten lords a'leaping, nine ladies dancing, eight maids a'milking, seven swans a'swimming, six geese a'laying, five gold rings! Four coly birds, three French hens, two turtle doves...

...And a partridge in a pear tree.